"That stupid Morgan! This is all his fault!" T.J. told himself as he got ready for bed. "Everything that's happened to me lately has been because of Morgan's stupid bet!"

T.J. angrily kicked his dresser, then sat down on the bed to rub his bruised foot. "I guess it really isn't all Morgan's fault," he finally admitted to himself. "I guess some of it is my fault for making that dumb bet in the first place."

Now everyone was mad at him and things would be worse in the morning. His teacher, Mrs. Tuttle, would find out about the rescue. So would all the other kids. They would be sure to laugh at him for it.

"Oh, I'd rather be dead than go to school tomorrow," T.J. groaned and fell back on his bed.

Other books by Nancy Simpson Levene

The T.J. Series
The Fastest Car in the County
The Pet That Never Was
Trouble in the Deep End
Hero for a Season
Master of Disaster

The ALEX Series
Shoelaces and Brussels Sprouts
French Fry Forgiveness
Hot Chocolate Friendship
Peanut Butter and Jelly Secrets
Mint Cookie Miracles
Cherry Cola Champions
The Salty Scarecrow Solution
Peach Pit Popularity
T-Bone Trouble
Grapefruit Basket Upset
Apple Turnover Treasure
Crocodile Meatloaf

*Chocolate Chips, Trumpet Tricks, and Other
Devotions with Alex*

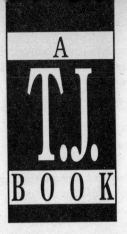

MASTER
OF DISASTER

NANCY   SIMPSON   LEVENE

Chariot Books™
A Division of Cook
Communications Ministries

Chariot Books™ is an imprint of Chariot Family Publishing
Cook Communications Ministries, Elgin, Illinois 60120
Cook Communications Ministries, Paris, Ontario
Kingsway Communications, Eastbourne, England

MASTER OF DISASTER
© 1995 by Nancy Simpson Levene for text and Robert Papp for illustrations

Scripture is from the New American Standard Bible, © the Lockman
Foundation 1960, 1962, 1963, 1968, 1971, 1972, 1973, 1975, 1977.

First printing, 1995
Printed in the United States of America
99 98 97 96 95 5 4 3 2 1

Library of Congress Cataloging-in-Publication Data
Levene, Nancy S., 1949-
Master of disaster / Nancy Simpson Levene.
p.   cm.
"A T.J. book"—Cover.
Summary: When T.J. loses a bet with Morgan Dover, the new boy in the third
grade, he is forced to be Morgan's slave for a week and finds himself in
trouble constantly.
ISBN 0-7814-0089-9
[1. Schools—Fiction. 2. Wagers—Fiction. 3. Christian life—Fiction.] I. Title.
PZ7.L5724Mas   1994
[Fic]—dc20
                                                    94-17356
                                                        CIP
                                                        AC

To Jesus,
Who enables His children
to prevail in battle
and
To Greg Land,
who boldly goes forth
to meet the giant.

And David put his hand into his bag and took from it a stone and slung it, and struck the Philistine on his forehead. And the stone sank into his forehead, so that he fell on his face to the ground.

I Samuel 17:49

ACKNOWLEDGMENTS

Thank you, Tom Cooper, for your friendship and for sharing your wealth of knowledge on the repair of doorknobs and other items. Thank you, Cara, for inspiring the doorknob caper, as well as contributing many other wonderful ideas, help, and support. (There is no better daughter.)

CONTENTS

1 The Bet   9
2 Backward Trouble   21
3 The Great Doorknob Caper   33
4 Rooftop Fugitives   45
5 An Awesome Rescue   57
6 Caught in the Act!   68
7 The Strongest Kind of Strong   76
8 Up Against the Giant!   86

1

THE BET

"Soccer players have to be really strong," T.J. bragged to the group of third grade boys on the school playground.

"Not as strong as wrestlers," argued a stout-looking boy. He stepped out of the crowd and looked T.J. in the eye. "Compared to wrestlers, soccer players are wimps!" he snarled.

"They are not!" hollered T.J. "Soccer players have it over wrestlers easy!"

"Oh yeah? Well, I'm a wrestler and I bet I'm a lot stronger than you are," said the boy.

"I bet you are not!" T.J. shot back.

"Okay, let's see who can do the most chin-ups on the top bar of the jungle gym," challenged the stout boy. "The winner gets to tell the loser what to do for the rest of the week. Is it a deal?"

"Sure, why not?" T.J. did not hesitate.

The two boys started toward the jungle gym,

their friends following close behind.

"T.J., you dummy!" whispered Zack, pulling his best friend to one side. "Don't you know who that big kid is? That's Morgan Dover. He just moved here from Chicago. His father's the new wrestling coach at the high school. Morgan works out with his dad every morning before school. You ought to see his muscles. I hate to tell you this, but you're gonna get creamed!"

T.J. pulled away from Zack. Even though Zack's words had worried him, he felt he had to look strong in front of the other guys.

Reaching the jungle gym, Morgan turned to T.J. "Do you want me to go first, Wimp?"

"Go ahead," T.J. said. "After you're finished, I'll show you how it's done."

"Fat chance!" Morgan laughed. He climbed up to the top bar of the jungle gym. The group of boys gathered around the bottom of the jungle gym to watch.

"We need an official counter," Morgan called to the boys.

"I'll do it!" cried a boy named Anthony. T.J. shook his head in disgust. Anthony had never really liked T.J. Now it looked as though he were eager to see T.J. get beat.

"I'd sure hate to be in your shoes, T.J.,"

whispered Aaron, a close friend of T.J.'s. The boys watched Morgan quickly and easily pull himself up and down, up and down, on the top bar. Anthony counted the chin-ups loudly, ". . . seven . . . eight . . . nine . . ."

T.J. held his breath. The last time he had tried a series of chin-ups, he had barely made it to twelve.

" . . . ten . . . eleven . . . twelve . . . "

Morgan doesn't even look tired! T.J. thought.

Finally, at twenty chin-ups, Morgan began to look tired. He made it past twenty-five, however, and ended the count at twenty-seven chin-ups.

"Wow!" the boys breathed. They all stared at Morgan as if he had just stepped out of a super-hero comic book.

T.J. felt sick. No way could he beat twenty-seven chin-ups. All the same, he climbed up the jungle gym. He would do as many chin-ups as he could before he passed out or died of a heart attack!

"Give it your best, T.J.!" Zack called from below.

After taking a couple of deep breaths, T.J. let his body hang from the top bar and began his chin-ups.

"One . . . two . . . three . . . " Anthony counted.

At first, T.J. tried to match Morgan's fast pace, but by number eight, he was slowing down. He forced his body to go on, to go up, down, up, down. He wasn't going to let Morgan win. Not if he could help it!

" . . . eleven . . . twelve . . . thirteen . . . " Anthony called.

Up, down, up, down. T.J.'s palms were sweating. It was hard to hang onto the bar. Up, down, up, down. His arms ached terribly.

T.J. had just made it past eighteen when it happened. His right hand slipped off the bar. He did not have the strength to hold on with one hand.

WOMP! T.J. fell off the bar and into the mud below, landing right at Morgan's feet.

"I won, Wimp!" Morgan said with a nasty grin. He and the other boys walked away.

"T.J., are you okay?" Zack asked his friend anxiously. He and Aaron dropped to their knees in the mud beside T.J.

"Yeah," T.J. groaned. "I guess you were right. I shouldn't have gone against Morgan Dover."

"Aw, don't feel bad," Zack replied. "None of the rest of us could have beaten him either."

"That's right," agreed Aaron.

"Nobody else was dumb enough to try," scowled T.J.

"Come on, recess is over," said Zack. "We gotta go back inside. Mrs. Tuttle is waving to us."

The three boys hurried toward their teacher who was waiting for them on the blacktop.

"Hurry up, boys, everyone else is inside," Mrs. Tuttle told them. "T.J., you are covered with mud! What happened?"

"Uh, I fell off the jungle gym," T.J. mumbled.

"Are you hurt?" the teacher asked.

"No, I'm okay," replied T.J.

"Well, then let's go inside," directed Mrs. Tuttle. She led Zack, Aaron, and T.J. back to the classroom.

After school, Zack and T.J. said good-bye to Aaron. Aaron had to go shopping with his mother.

Zack and T.J. then met T.J.'s younger brother, Charley, and headed out the front door of the school. Suddenly a hand grabbed T.J. from behind.

"Hey, Wimp! Where d'ya think you're going?" Morgan Dover hissed in T.J.'s ear.

"The name is T.J., not Wimp," replied T.J., angrily brushing the bigger boy's hand off his arm.

"Okay, T.J.," Morgan said smugly. "You lost the bet we made, remember? You gotta do whatever I tell you to do for the rest of the week."

"That's right," cried Anthony. He and several other boys ran to stand beside Morgan. "We all heard the bet."

T.J. looked at Zack miserably. Zack shrugged and looked down at the ground.

"Okay," T.J. said. "You won the bet. What do you want me to do?"

"Tomorrow I want you to wear all your clothes backward to school," Morgan said with a grin. "Wear your shirt backward and your pants backward. Wear your shoes on the wrong feet. You also have to walk backward!"

The crowd of boys hooted at Morgan's words. It sounded so funny that even T.J. had to smile.

"But my mom won't let me come to school with my clothes on backward," T.J. told Morgan.

"Then come to school early and put your clothes on backward in the rest room," suggested Anthony loudly.

"Thanks a lot, Anthony," T.J. muttered.

"See you tomorrow, Wimp," said Morgan. He and the others walked away.

"How can I wear my clothes backward and walk backward for a whole day?" T.J. asked Zack.

"I dunno, but I guess you'll have to try," Zack answered. "After all, Morgan won the bet."

"Yeah, I know," T.J. sighed. "Why was I stupid enough to make that bet with Morgan?"

"Come on," Zack said as he clapped his friend on the back. "At least it's only for the rest of the week."

"Yeah, but today's only Monday," T.J. said gloomily.

When they got home, T.J. said to Zack, "Come up to my room and help me find some clothes that I can wear backward tomorrow."

"Okay, just let me go tell my mom I'm home from school," Zack replied. He hurried across the yard to his own house. Zack lived next door to T.J. The two boys had been best friends for as long as they could remember.

T.J. and Zack lived on a little tree-lined street named Maple. It was a short street that ended in a circle. Hardly any cars came down the street, so the boys could skateboard, roller-blade, or ride bikes without fear of traffic.

Inside his house, T.J. waited impatiently for Zack to return. While he waited, he was surprised to discover his father in the family room. Father was down on his hands and knees beside the outside door that led to the backyard. His tool box sat nearby. The lid was open and tools were scattered around on the floor.

"Why are you home so early, Dad?" T.J. asked.

"Oh, I thought I'd come home early today to do a few chores around the house," Father explained to T.J. "I'm getting ready to replace the doorknob on this door."

"Good!" T.J. approved. "That door is too hard to open."

"That's just what your mother says," replied Father with a smile. "She's been after me to fix it for a long time. Would you like to be my assistant?"

"I would help you, but Zack's coming over," T.J. told his father regretfully. He loved to help his father fix things around the house.

"He doesn't need your help!" Charley cried, suddenly stumbling into the room. "I'm gonna be Dad's assistant!"

T.J. and Father stared at Charley. The first grader was dressed in an old pair of T.J.'s overalls that were two sizes too big for him. The pockets of the overalls were stuffed with tools. A hammer hung from one of the pockets, while several screwdrivers and a wrench protruded from the others. A baseball cap sat backward on top of Charley's head, but what made T.J. and Father laugh was the pair of oversized sports goggles Charley wore on his face.

"Aren't those my racquetball goggles?" Father asked his younger son.

"Yep," Charley admitted. "Repairmen should protect their eyes from splinters and, you know, metal stuff like nails that might fly into their eyes."

"Oh," Father nodded. He reached out and caught Charley as the little boy stumbled and tripped over Father's feet. "I think those goggles might be more of a hazard than a help if they keep you from seeing clearly," said Father.

T.J. laughed. Charley was such a crack-up! He always had to know how things worked. He took apart everything he could get his hands on, and then tried to put it back together again, sometimes not too successfully. T.J. had lost a good train engine that way.

"Well, I gotta go," T.J. told his father as the doorbell suddenly rang.

"Come on upstairs," T.J. said to Zack as soon as

he had opened the door. The two boys ran up the two flights of stairs to T.J.'s bedroom on the third floor.

T.J.'s room was the only one on the third floor, and the highest in the house. T.J. called it his loft bedroom. It was a long rectangular room with a row of double windows on one side. In one corner of the room stood a bunk bed. In another stood a raised platform supporting an intricate model train layout, complete with mountains, tunnels, bridges, and a village.

As soon as he entered the room, Zack ran straight to the train table and threw a switch. A bright yellow Union Pacific engine came to life.

"Let's turn off the lights and watch the train lights in the dark," suggested Zack.

"First, we have to decide what clothes I can wear backward tomorrow," T.J. reminded his friend.

"Oh yeah," Zack studied T.J.'s clothes.

"You don't want to wear a shirt with a collar like that," said Zack, pointing to a red and white striped rugby shirt.

"Right," T.J. agreed. "Also, sweat pants would be easier to wear backward than jeans."

"Oh yeah," Zack said. "Jeans would be a killer to put on backward."

"Okay, then it's settled," T.J. said happily. "I'll just wear my soccer sweats to school. Maybe nobody will even be able to tell that they're on backward!"

The next morning, however, T.J. ran into a difficulty he had not expected. As soon as he appeared at the breakfast table, Mother exclaimed, "T.J., you're not planning to wear your soccer sweats to school, are you?"

"Sure, why not?" T.J. asked.

"Because they are worn and grubby-looking with grass stains on the knees," Mother replied. "Go back upstairs and put on some jeans and a better-looking shirt."

"But, Mom . . . " T.J. tried to protest.

"T.J., do as your mother says and do it quickly," ordered Father sternly. "We will wait breakfast for you."

Climbing back up the two flights of stairs to his bedroom, T.J. threw off his sweats and yanked on a pair of blue jeans. He took a blue T-shirt out of his dresser drawer and put it on. Then he ran downstairs to the kitchen.

"T.J., that is not what I would call a better-looking shirt," Mother stared at the blue T-shirt.

"Aw, Mom, give me a break," T.J. cried, frustrated that his plan to find something easy to wear backward was quickly falling apart.

"T.J., that is no way to speak to your mother," said Father sternly.

Sliding into his chair at the table, T.J. ducked his head and hoped that his mother would let the matter drop; but as soon as the blessing was said and the food was served, Mother disappeared from the room. T.J. heard her footsteps on the stairs. Two minutes later, she returned with T.J.'s red and white striped rugby shirt in her hand.

"You can wear this shirt to school today, T.J.," Mother said in her no-nonsense voice.

T.J. did not even try to argue. After breakfast, he changed shirts and left the house with his brother, Charley.

I'm in for it now, he thought as he and Charley waited for Zack. *With blue jeans and a collar on my shirt, Mrs. Tuttle is bound to notice when they are on backward. I'll probably get in tons of trouble!*

2

BACKWARD TROUBLE

When T.J. and Zack arrived at school, they said good-bye to Charley and then ducked into the nearest boys' rest room.

"I can't believe your mom made you wear that rugby shirt," Zack said as T.J. threw off his jacket and hurried into a stall. "That shirt is the absolute worst one to try and wear backward!"

"I know," T.J. moaned from inside the stall. He pulled his arms out of the sleeves, and then pulled the shirt around his neck so that the front side was to the back and the back side to his front. He stuck his arms back into the sleeves and pulled the shirt down over his stomach.

"Yuuuck! This feels terrible!" T.J. hollered. "The collar is choking me."

T.J. took off his jeans. He turned them around and stepped into them backward so that the zipper was at the rear and the two back pockets at the front.

"Help!" T.J. cried. "I can't pull up the zipper!"

Grinning from ear to ear, Zack stepped into the bathroom stall with T.J. With some difficulty, he closed the top snap of T.J.'s jeans, and then grabbed hold of the bottom part of the zipper and yanked hard.

"Hold still!" Zack ordered as T.J. lurched forward, grabbing hold of the toilet seat in front of him for support.

Zack jerked mightily on the zipper. The humor of the situation suddenly struck T.J., and he began to laugh. Zack joined him, and soon the boys were laughing so hard that tears rolled down their faces.

All at once, the outside door to the bathroom swung open. Aaron, Morgan, and several other boys entered the bathroom. They took one look at Zack and T.J. and broke into howls of laughter.

With the combined help of his friends, T.J. managed to get the zipper pulled up on his jeans. The boys then supported T.J. as they switched his shoes, putting the right one on his left foot and the left one on his right foot.

"I don't think I can walk," T.J. gasped.

Two boys grabbed T.J.'s arms. They turned

him around and propelled him backward out of the bathroom door and backward down the hallway to their classroom.

The hall was crowded with noisy children. Everyone stopped and stared at T.J.

"Look at T.J.!" giggled several girls.

"Get me outta here!" T.J. groaned. He covered his eyes with his hands.

The boys pulled T.J. to the classroom door, but there they left him. They all rushed to their seats to get there before the late bell rang.

"Hey! Come back here!" T.J. cried. He lurched into the classroom, lost his balance, and tumbled to the floor. Getting up on his hands and knees, he walked backward in crab-like fashion to his desk. He hurriedly pulled himself up into the seat just as the bell rang.

The class exploded with cheers and hilarious laughter at T.J.'s performance. Red-faced, T.J. stole a glance at his teacher, Mrs. Tuttle. The teacher sat at her desk and stared back at T.J. without smiling. T.J. quickly ducked his head.

Mrs. Tuttle did not say a word as she waited for the class to settle down. It did not take long. The room fell silent under her steady gaze.

"Take out your spelling workbooks," said Mrs. Tuttle in a quiet but firm voice.

Everyone hurried to obey. T.J. looked around at his friends in surprise. Wasn't Mrs. Tuttle going to yell at him?

To everyone's amazement, Mrs. Tuttle completely ignored T.J. She would call on everyone but him to answer her questions.

Squirming in his chair, T.J. spent the most uncomfortable two hours of his life. The collar of the rugby shirt pulled chokingly tight against his throat. The seat of his blue jeans, with its two bulky pockets, bunched up around his middle, while the front zipper pulled and pinched him from behind.

His clothes, however, were not his first worry. He was most concerned about his teacher. Why was Mrs. Tuttle ignoring him? Did she not like him anymore? T.J. hated that idea. He was a good student and had always gotten along with his teachers.

When morning recess finally arrived, the children lined up at the door—everyone, that is, but T.J. Mrs. Tuttle had asked him to remain seated.

After the other children had gone, Mrs. Tuttle walked over to T.J.'s desk and stared down at T.J. for what seemed like a long time.

"Does your mother know how you dressed for school today?" Mrs. Tuttle asked T.J. at last.

"No," T.J. mumbled.

"Did you turn your clothes around backward after you got to school?" the teacher asked.

"Yes, in the rest room," squeaked T.J.

"Why?" Mrs. Tuttle wanted to know.

T.J. was silent. If he told his teacher about his bet with Morgan, he would be a tattletale.

"I guess I was just trying to be funny," T.J. finally told the teacher.

"I do not think that wearing your clothes backward to school is very funny," Mrs. Tuttle said sternly. "Don't do it again."

"Okay," T.J. quickly agreed.

"As punishment, you will miss both of your recesses today," said the teacher. "If you ever do this again, you will be taken to the principal's office. Do you understand?"

"Yes, Ma'am," T.J. said as he ducked his head.

"Now, go to the rest room and put your clothes on the proper way!" ordered Mrs. Tuttle.

T.J. jumped to his feet and tried to scramble from the room, but because his shoes were on the wrong feet and his pants were on backward, he only succeeded in diving headfirst to the floor.

Mrs. Tuttle helped T.J. to his feet. She took off T.J.'s shoes and handed them to him.

"You had better carry your shoes to the rest room," the teacher told him. "It's safer that way."

After school, T.J., Zack, and Aaron hurried toward the front door of the school building.

"T.J.!" a voice shouted. "Come back here!"

"Oh no, not again!" T.J. moaned. "Quick! Let's make it outside before Morgan catches up to us."

"Oops, no such luck," T.J. muttered as he and his friends bumped headfirst into the group of third-grade boys.

"You wouldn't be thinking about running out on Morgan, would you, T.J.?" Anthony said with a smirk as he and the others stepped up to block T.J.'s way.

"Uh, no," T.J. sighed. "Whatever gave you that idea?"

"Anthony, why don't you mind your own business?" Zack exclaimed, clenching his fists.

Anthony, always tough in word but not in deed, quickly stepped backward out of Zack's reach.

Just then, Morgan reached the group. Stepping in front of T.J., Morgan said, "You can't leave school until I say so. You have to do whatever I say for the rest of the week, remember?"

"I'm not wearing my clothes backward any more!" T.J. said hotly. "I got in lots of trouble with Mrs. Tuttle."

"We know!" Morgan and the other boys laughed.

"I'll tell you what," Morgan said after the laughter had died down. "We will think up something extra fun for you to do tomorrow. We'll tell you about it in the morning."

"I can hardly wait," T.J. sighed. "Can I go now? My little brother is waiting for me outside."

"Sure, go find your little brother," sneered Morgan. He let T.J. exit the building.

"Sayonara!" Anthony called after them.

"That Anthony!" Zack punched one fist into the palm of his other hand. "I'd like to pound him!"

"I'd like to pound all of them," T.J. replied.

"Yeah, some friends!" declared Aaron.

The boys met T.J.'s brother, Charley, and the four of them walked home.

"Let's get some kids together and play soccer," T.J. suggested to Zack and Aaron. "I'd like to do something to get my mind off all the trouble I got into today."

"Okay," the boys readily agreed.

When T.J. went inside to change clothes, he asked Charley if he would like to play soccer.

"No, sorry," Charley responded. "Charley's Repair Service has a job to do."

"Huh?" T.J. scratched his head, puzzled at Charley's reply. Shrugging, T.J. went outside to meet Zack and Aaron. Several children in the neighborhood joined them, and soon they had an exciting game underway.

By the time Mother called T.J. to come inside, he had scored eight goals and felt tremendously better. His team had beaten Zack's by one goal.

"T.J., please change out of those muddy sweat pants," Mother said as soon as she saw him. "We'll be eating in just a few minutes."

Dashing up the stairs two at a time, T.J. reached his bedroom only to find Charley down on his hands and knees in front of T.J.'s bedroom door. The door was closed. Tools and metal pieces littered the stairway landing.

"Charley, what's going on?" T.J. exclaimed, smelling trouble.

"Now, T.J., don't get excited," the seven year old said in a rush. "Charley's Repair Service will get everything all fixed in a jiffy."

"Get all what fixed?" T.J. frowned.

"The doorknob," Charley replied. He pulled a screwdriver out of one of his overall pockets.

"What do you mean 'the doorknob'?" T.J. cried loudly. He studied his bedroom door. Where the doorknob used to be was now a gaping hole.

"Oh no!" T.J. collapsed to the floor and held his head in his hands.

"Don't worry, Charley's Repair Service will fix it in no time," said Charley. "Trust me."

T.J. glared at his younger brother. He might have known Charley would pull a stunt like this after watching Father fix the doorknob on the family room door.

"Why'd you pick my door?" T.J. asked Charley.

"Easy! Yours is the only one way up here by itself. Mom would never let me take a doorknob off of a door downstairs," replied Charley.

"No kidding," T.J. mumbled. "Let me into my room. I gotta change clothes."

"You can't. The door won't open without the doorknob," Charley looked at his older brother as if T.J. were the dumbest person on earth for not knowing such a thing.

"You can't just push it open?" T.J. asked.

"Not when the door's closed and the doorknob is off," Charley retorted.

"But you had to open the door to get the doorknob off in the first place, didn't you?" T.J. gritted his teeth. He was trying very hard not to haul off and clobber Charley.

"Yeah, it was open when I took off the doorknob," Charley admitted.

"Then why did you close it before you got it back together again?" T.J. wanted to know.

Charley shrugged his shoulders. "Guess it's more of a challenge this way."

T.J. slapped the top of the stairway railing hard. He sat down heavily on the top step of the stairway and tried to get his anger under control.

"Well, you had better get it fixed and get it fixed fast!" T.J. hissed. "And just remember, from now on, you are not allowed to mess with any of my stuff, including my doorknob!"

Before Charley had a chance to answer, a sudden high-pitched whine, followed by a bark, sounded from behind T.J.'s closed door. The two boys stared at one another.

"Oh no!" they cried. "Sergeant's in there!"

T.J. rushed to the door. He put his face up to the hole where the doorknob should have been, and stared through it into his bedroom. There, a few feet away, and staring back at him with the most pitiful expression on his face, sat his large German shepherd, Sergeant.

"Way to go, Charley!" exclaimed T.J. "You locked the dog in my bedroom."

"Uh, sorry, Sarge. We'll have you out in a jiffy!" Charley called to the dog.

"Woof!" came the reply.

"We gotta get this fixed so we can let Sergeant out," T.J. declared. "I'll help."

The two boys worked feverishly, trying their best to fit the doorknob back into the hole in the door.

"This isn't working," T.J. said finally. "We need the door open. Then we can hold the doorknob in place from the other side while we screw it on."

"Okay," Charley sighed. "Be my guest." He motioned for T.J. to try and open the door.

T.J. felt all around inside the hole. "There's gotta be something you push to unlatch the door, but I can't find it."

Just then, what T.J. had been dreading happened. Mother called up the stairs, "It's time for dinner!"

"Oh great! Now what are we gonna do?" T.J. hissed. "The door is stuck. Sergeant's locked in my bedroom. I still have on my muddy clothes, and now Mom's calling us to dinner!"

3

THE GREAT DOORKNOB CAPER

When Mother called them to dinner, T.J. and Charley dropped the doorknob parts and tools to the floor. Doorknob fixing would have to wait.

"Don't worry, Boy, we'll be back," T.J. called to his dog, Sergeant, through the hole in the door.

"Woof!" Sergeant whined. He pawed at the door.

"Sergeant, lie down," T.J. ordered. He watched through the hole as Sergeant plopped down heavily on the floor near the door.

"This isn't going to work," T.J. told Charley. "He'll probably make a racket while we're eating dinner. We could get in a lot of trouble, you know."

The boys ran downstairs to the dining room. The rest of the family had already taken their places at the table.

"You boys need to go wash your hands," Mother said. "T.J., didn't I tell you to change out of those muddy sweat pants? Get a towel from the kitchen. You can spread it over your chair."

T.J. and Charley ran to wash their hands. When they returned, the blessing was said. They had hardly taken their first bite, however, before loud barking sounded from upstairs.

"Sounds like Sergeant got locked in a closet or something," Father remarked.

"I thought somebody was missing!" Mother exclaimed. "The dog's not here, begging for food."

"T.J., please go see what is the matter with the dog," Father said as Sergeant continued to bark.

The boys exchanged panicky glances.

"Sergeant's okay," T.J. spoke up. "He's just up in my room."

"Well, he sounds like he is trapped or something. Did you shut him up in your room?" Father asked.

"Well, uh, not exactly," T.J. stammered. "At least, I didn't mean to."

"Why don't you go see what's wrong with Sergeant?" Mother suggested. "Bring him downstairs so we can eat our dinner in peace."

"But Mom, there's nothing wrong with Sergeant," T.J. insisted.

At that moment, extra loud barks erupted from upstairs. T.J. glared at his brother. This was all Charley's fault.

"T.J.! Go see about that dog immediately!"
Father ordered.

Sighing heavily, T.J. left the table and ran up
the two flights of stairs to his bedroom. He slid on
his knees across the landing to the bedroom
door. Peeking through the doorknob hole, T.J.
tried to reason with Sergeant.

"Look, Boy, you're getting me in trouble. Can't
you be quiet for a while?"

Sergeant whined and tried to stick his nose
into the hole. He pawed at the door.

"Sergeant," T.J. tried again, "you're not
missing much. The table scraps are not that great.
We're only having chicken. Look, if you don't
bark any more, I'll give you a whole peanut butter
sandwich when Mom's not looking."

"Woof!" Sergeant seemed to like that idea.

"Okay, Boy, please keep quiet," T.J. begged. "I
will be back after dinner and get you out."

Hurrying back downstairs, T.J. heard Sergeant
whine and cry at the door. "This is hopeless," T.J.
told himself. "I oughta pulverize that Charley!"

"Okay, where's Sergeant?" Father asked as
soon as T.J. had returned to the dining room.

"He's okay," T.J. replied, trying to appear calm.
"He's in my room. He likes it up there."

"Yeah," Charley spoke up, trying his best to

help out the situation. "Sometimes he stays up in T.J.'s room by himself for hours and hours."

"Hmmmmpf!" sniffed Mother. "Not at dinnertime!"

As if to prove her point, loud barking began again from upstairs.

Father looked from one boy to the other. "Okay," he said, getting up and throwing his napkin on the table. "I'll see about Sergeant myself."

"Oh no, Dad," both T.J. and Charley cried. They ran after Father, taking the stairs two at a time to keep up with Father's long strides.

"What is going on here?" Father demanded as soon as he reached the landing outside T.J.'s bedroom door. "Who took my toolbox and spread the tools out all over the floor?"

T.J. and Charley stood silently and stared at the floor.

"I want an answer," Father ordered.

T.J. nudged Charley. Finally, after a long minute of silence, the younger boy confessed.

"Charley's Repair Service was called in to fix an especially troublesome doorknob," Charley told his father with the tiniest of hopeful smiles on his face.

Father stared down at his younger son. "I believe Charley's Repair Service is about to go out of business!" he said. "What do you mean a troublesome doorknob?" He studied T.J.'s bedroom door. "Don't tell me you took off the doorknob!" he groaned.

"Yeah, Dad, that's what he did," T.J. spoke up. "But he didn't know Sergeant was in there when he shut the door."

By now, Sergeant was barking furiously, hearing all the voices outside the door.

Mother appeared on the stairway with T.J.'s little sisters, Megan and Elizabeth. The two little girls laughed and hopped all around the landing.

Ignoring everyone, Father searched the floor for a screwdriver. Finding one, he pushed it into the hole in T.J.'s door and twisted clockwise. Presto! The door, released from the plate in the wall, swung open immediately. Out sprang a joyful Sergeant, glad to be released from his prison.

Father motioned for everyone to go back downstairs. They trooped down the stairs and, once again, took their places at the dining room table. Sergeant took his place between T.J. and Elizabeth. He had picked this spot as T.J. usually slipped the dog a few scraps under cover, while three-year-old Elizabeth was known to out-and-out throw things from her plate to the floor.

"Well," Father said, "Thank you, Charley and T.J., for a most entertaining dinner activity, one we could have all done without!"

"It wasn't me!" T.J. blurted out. "Charley took off the doorknob and locked Sergeant in my bedroom. I had nothing to do with it."

"You are not completely innocent," Father gave T.J. a stern look. "When I first asked you about Sergeant, you did not tell me that he was locked in your room."

"Sorry," T.J. hung his head. "I was just trying to keep Charley out of trouble."

"And did it keep Charley out of trouble?" Father asked.

"No," T.J. admitted. "It didn't even keep me out of trouble."

Father nodded. "I think it caused you more trouble than you would have had by telling me the truth in the first place. When will you boys learn to admit when you have done something wrong, rather than to try and hide it? Problems always get bigger when you cover them up. It's better to deal with them out in the open.

"After dinner, you boys can help me put the doorknob back on T.J.'s door," Father continued. "You will stay in your room after school tomorrow and there will be no evening television tonight or tomorrow night. From now on, I do not want Charley's Repair Service to fix anything in the house unless I know about it first. Is that understood, Charley?"

"Yes, Dad," Charley answered meekly.

T.J. sighed. His little brother had such an amazing talent for getting himself—and T.J.—in trouble. What would he think of next?

"Uh, Dad," Charley spoke up a moment later. "Does not fixing things include the toaster?"

Father put down his fork and stared at Charley. T.J. gulped.

"What do you mean?" Father asked Charley in a very suspicious tone of voice.

"Well, I kinda fixed the toaster this afternoon before I fixed the doorknob," Charley admitted.

"But Charley," Mother interjected, "there was nothing wrong with the toaster."

"Uh, I wanted to see if I could make the toast pop out higher," Charley tried to explain.

"And did you succeed?" Father asked, resting his head in his hands and looking very tired.

"Yeah, I think so," Charley replied.

Mother rose from her chair and went to the kitchen for the toaster. Plugging it into a wall outlet, she stuck a piece of bread into the toaster and waited.

The family held its breath to see what would happen. It didn't take long. Suddenly, after a loud click, the piece of toast rocketed out of the toaster and hit the ceiling fan above the dining room table. Showers of crumbs flew all over as the toast fell PLOP! to the center of the table.

Mother and Father silently stared at Charley with their mouths wide open, while T.J. and his two younger sisters fell to the floor and rolled around, laughing long and hard.

That night, after prayers were said and the lights were out, T.J. lay awake for a long while. Too much had happened that day for him to fall asleep easily. He had had trouble all day—at school when he wore his clothes backward and got in trouble with Mrs. Tuttle, and then at home with Charley and the doorknob episode.

"I sure hope tomorrow is better," he told himself.

Rolling over, T.J. was about to fall asleep when a sudden thought struck him. Tomorrow might be equally bad. Hadn't Morgan said that he and the guys would think up something extra fun for T.J. to do? T.J. groaned. He could be sure of one thing. It might be extra fun for Morgan and the others, but it wouldn't be fun for T.J.!

The next morning, as T.J., Zack, Aaron, and Charley were crossing the street in front of the school, T.J. gasped and pointed at the schoolyard. "Look!"

There on the sidewalk by the front steps, stood a familiar-looking group of boys. It was Morgan, Anthony, and the other third-grade boys.

"I'm done for," T.J. muttered.

"Maybe we can sneak around to the side door of the school," Zack quickly suggested.

T.J. sighed. "Too late. They've spotted me."

True to his words, the boys across the street began to wave and call to T.J. Morgan stood in their midst, arms folded, a wicked grin on his face.

As T.J. approached the group, several of the boys pointed at him and giggled.

"Hi, Slave," Anthony greeted T.J.

"Are you talking to me?" T.J. growled.

"Yeah, you're our slave, T.J.," taunted Anthony. "You have to do everything we say."

"I don't have to do anything you say, Anthony," T.J. replied. "I only have to do what Morgan says."

"And I say you are going to be our slave," Morgan stepped up to stand in front of T.J.

"But . . ." T.J. began.

"He's right, T.J.," the other boys hollered. "You made the bet, and a bet is a bet!"

"Okay, okay," T.J. sighed. "I'll be your slave for three more days. Come on, we're all going to be late for school if we stand out here any longer."

"Just a minute, Slave," Morgan held him back. "A slave walks ten paces behind his masters."

"Okay, then go in ahead of me," replied T.J., standing back to let the others move in front of him.

"A slave carries things for his masters," Morgan grinned, and handed T.J. his lunch box and jacket.

The other boys whooped in glee. They rushed at T.J., handing him jackets, lunch boxes, and books to carry. T.J. was so loaded down, he could barely fit through the front door of the school.

The group of boys pranced on ahead as T.J. stumbled down the halls of the school with his burden. Zack and Aaron marched helplessly along. T.J. had no problem keeping ten paces behind the other boys. He lagged further and further behind, hampered by falling items that he had to continually stop to pick up.

"We better hurry," Aaron worried. "I think it's really late. The halls are getting real empty."

"Yeah," T.J. groaned. "After yesterday, I don't need to get into any more trouble."

"Can't you go any faster?" Zack cried.

"Not with all this stuff," T.J. gasped.

"Just three rooms to go, T.J.," Aaron tried to encourage his friend. By now, the hall was completely empty.

"Thanks, you guys. Thanks for sticking with me," T.J. replied, grateful for such loyal friends.

"Aw, you'd do the same for us," Zack replied. "Come on, we're almost there. Let's go for it!"

His arms wrapped tightly around the odd bundle of items he carried, T.J. tore down the hall with his friends. They reached the door just as the bell began to ring.

Rushing through the doorway, T.J. tripped and rolled on the floor. Lunch boxes, books, and jackets slid this way and that as they hit the floor and crashed into the first two rows of students' desks. One lunch box slid into Mrs. Tutttle's desk, banging hard on her chair.

T.J. rolled to a stop right under his teacher's feet. He looked up at Mrs. Tuttle's frowning face.

Oh boy, thought T.J., *here we go again!*

4

ROOFTOP FUGITIVES

"T.J.!" Mrs. Tuttle cried. "What are you doing?"

"Uh, I was trying to carry all this stuff, and I guess I tripped," T.J. replied, scrambling to his feet. He rubbed a bruise on his elbow.

"Why are you carrying so many coats, lunch boxes, and books?" his teacher wanted to know.

"Oh, well, uh, I dunno," T.J. stammered, hanging his head and not knowing what to say.

"Because he's our slave!" someone shouted. Twitters and giggles filled the classroom.

Mrs. Tuttle frowned and the noises stopped. The teacher held up a jacket. "Whose is this?" she asked.

Slowly, Anthony raised his hand.

"Come here and get your jacket," the teacher told Anthony. "Go hang it in the coat closet."

Anthony shuffled to the front of the room and took his jacket from Mrs. Tuttle.

"If these jackets and other items belong to

anyone here, come and claim them now," said Mrs. Tuttle, "or I will take them to the lost and found."

The boys in the classroom hurried to collect their belongings from the teacher.

When they had all finally returned to their desks, Mrs. Tuttle said, "I am tired of this nonsense. If there is any further trouble in this classroom, I will call the principal to settle it."

T.J. squirmed under the teacher's sharp gaze. He had been the main one in trouble. If anyone were to be sent to the principal's office, it would be him.

At recess, Morgan and the other boys followed T.J. around the playground.

"Hey, Slave!" they called to T.J. Finally, T.J. could stand it no more. Turning to face the others, he said, "Go away! Leave me alone!"

"We don't have to, Slave," taunted Anthony.

"Say that to me some time when we're alone, Anthony," T.J. raised his fists.

"Yeah, some time when you don't have all the other guys to protect you," added Zack.

"Well, T.J. is our slave," insisted Anthony, stepping back a pace or two. "Morgan said so."

"That's right," Morgan spoke up. "You made a bet, remember?" he asked T.J.

"I'm not doing anything that'll get me in more trouble with Mrs. Tuttle," declared T.J.

"Okay," agreed Morgan. "I know something that won't get you in trouble."

"What?" T.J. asked suspiciously.

"Go play with the girls on the jungle gym," Morgan replied with a big grin. "I want to see you hang from your knees and do flips off the bars."

The other boys laughed at Morgan's command.

"Aw, come on," T.J. whined. "I can't do that."

"Go on," Morgan ordered. "You lost the bet. Now you have to do what I say."

"Yeah, T.J.," the boys chanted, "a bet is a bet!"

"I'm going! I'm going!" T.J. sighed. The boys laughed loudly as T.J. made his way to the jungle gym. He sat on one of the lower bars.

Morgan followed T.J. "Climb up to that bar," Morgan pointed to an empty bar smack dab in the center of the girls' territory. Two girls hung from their knees on either side of it.

"You gotta be kidding!" T.J. exclaimed.

"Get going!" Morgan said with a grin. "We'll see how many tricks you can do on the bars."

Slowly, T.J. climbed to the top of the jungle gym and sat on the bar between Ashley McKeever and Jennifer Shull. He hoped the girls would not notice him.

"T.J.! What are you doing here?" Ashley squinted one eye and glared at him from her upside-down position.

"Uh . . . nothing," T.J. mumbled.

"T.J., you're such a nerd!" sighed Jennifer from the other side of T.J. Lifting her legs off the bar, Jennifer raised herself to a handstand position. Even in that position, Jennifer managed to toss her long blonde hair, resembling a miniature movie star. T.J. shifted uncomfortably on the bar.

"What's the matter, T.J.?" the boys laughed from below.

"Why don't you kiss Jennifer?" one boy hollered.

"Yeah, T.J., Jennifer wants you to kiss her!"

"Shut up!" T.J. shouted down at the boys.

The girls giggled.

"Oh, T.J., won't you come over and sit on my bar?" teased one girl.

"T.J., come sit over here!" called another.

Immediately, all the girls took up the cry. T.J. ducked his head and felt his face turn bright red.

Desperately, he slid off the bar and half-fell, half-jumped to the ground. The taunts of the girls and the laughter of the boys filled his ears as he stumbled away from the jungle gym as fast as he could go. Zack and Aaron ran after him.

T.J. did not stop running until he reached the farthest corner of the playground. Then he collapsed to the ground. His friends fell down beside him.

"I never want to see any of those creeps again! Never!" T.J. gasped.

"You mean the boys or the girls?" Aaron asked.

"All of them," T.J. replied. "They're all jerks!"

"No kidding," Zack agreed, "but unless you change schools or something, you're gonna have to see 'em again."

"Yeah," said T.J. glumly. He sat at the far corner of the playground until recess was over.

At the end of the school day, Mrs. Tuttle reminded her students, "Don't forget to bring a shoe box to school tomorrow. We need to decorate them so they will be ready for Valentine's Day on Friday. Remember to buy enough valentines to give one to every person in the class."

"Yeah!" cried the girls. They chatted about the different ways to decorate their shoe boxes.

"I'm going to put pink roses all over my shoe box," declared one girl.

"I'm going to draw candy hearts that say 'CUTIE PIE' and 'LET'S KISS,' on mine" said another girl.

The girls all laughed.

T.J. groaned. Valentines were okay if they had dinosaurs or basketball players on them. But most valentines were too mushy and stupid.

When the bell rang to end school, T.J. and Zack rushed out the door. They waved good-bye to Aaron who was walking home with another friend. T.J. and Zack turned to the right instead of their usual left, and ducked around a corner into the school library. Cautiously, they peeked around the library door to look back at their classroom.

"There's Morgan!" T.J. warned in a low voice.

"And Anthony," whispered Zack.

T.J. and Zack watched as Morgan, Anthony, and their friends turned left out of the classroom door and hurried down the hallway.

"They're looking for me," said T.J.

"Good! Let 'em look! Let's go!" hissed Zack.

Zack and T.J. raced down the hall in the opposite direction from Morgan and Anthony. They met Charley at the back door of the building.

"Come on, Charley, run!" T.J. called to his younger brother as he and Zack neared the door.

Charley did not hesitate but quickly raced out the door after the two older boys.

"There they go!" a voice cried behind them.

T.J. glanced back over his shoulder. "Oh no! They've spotted us! Morgan and the others are coming after us!"

"Quick, follow me!" Zack shouted. He led T.J. and Charley around the corner of the building and back into a small alcove. It led to an inner courtyard where a separate playground for the kindergartners was located.

"The gate's locked!" T.J. cried as he tried to

open the gate to the courtyard. He looked around, panic-stricken. The sound of pounding footsteps could be heard not far behind.

"Climb over the fence!" Zack hissed.

The three boys climbed quickly. Zack and T.J. made it over with no trouble, but Charley got stuck!

"Help!" Charley cried. One of his pant legs had caught on the spikes of the metal fence.

T.J. and Zack worked frantically to free Charley. They twisted, pulled, and finally jerked with all their might. RIP! POP! The pants came free and Charley fell off the fence into the older boys' arms. They quickly threw themselves behind a row of bushes, just a moment before the group of boys, with Morgan in the lead, reached the alcove that led to the courtyard.

"Hey, do you think they went in there?" T.J. heard Anthony shout.

The boys advanced through the alcove to the courtyard fence. Morgan shook the gate.

"Naw, they didn't go in there," he said. "The gate's locked."

"They could've climbed over the fence," insisted Anthony.

"Do you see them?" Morgan asked.

"No sign of them," the boys told Morgan.

"Let's go! They're probably on the other side of the building by now," Morgan said.

The group of boys took off at a run—all but Anthony. T.J. and Zack grimaced as they watched the heavyset boy peer suspiciously into the courtyard.

"Oh no, he's coming in!" whispered T.J. as Anthony awkwardly began to climb the fence.

"Don't worry, the three of us can take him," said Zack in a low voice, looking pleased with the idea.

That opportunity never came, for just as Charley had become stuck on the top part of the fence, so did Anthony.

"Ouch! Oh, somebody help!" bawled Anthony. He tried again and again to kick himself free.

T.J., Zack, and Charley controlled their giggles as they witnessed Anthony's battle with the fence. Finally, with a loud ripping sound, Anthony fell backward to the ground. He limped away slowly, one pant leg torn open and flapping in the wind.

Crawling out from the bushes, the boys wiped the laughter tears from their eyes. T.J. had laughed so hard at Anthony that his stomach hurt.

Remaining silent, the boys crept back to the fence. They peered through the alcove. All seemed quiet. This time, Zack and T.J. helped Charley to climb back over the fence.

The three boys crept back through the alcove. T.J. took the lead. He motioned Zack and Charley to follow him as he started off in the opposite direction of Morgan and the boys.

"How about hiding down at the bottom of those steps?" T.J. asked Zack. They had come upon a deep outside stairwell that led to the basement of the school.

"Naw, that's a dead end," frowned Zack. "They'd catch us for sure."

"We gotta hide somewhere," T.J. worried. "They'll be coming around again real soon."

"Yeah, I know," Zack frowned. Then his eyes lit up. "Hey, look over there! Let's go up that ladder!"

T.J. looked to see a long ladder that leaned against the side of the school building, leading up to the roof. It looked like just the kind of place to go and disappear from sight.

The three boys ran over to the ladder and hurriedly raced up its rungs. Climbing onto the school roof, they congratulated each other on finding such a wonderful place to hide. A raised metal box containing what looked like a fan with large blades stood nearby. They crawled behind it, laid low, and waited.

They did not have to wait long. Soon the sound of shrill voices and pounding feet could be heard directly below them.

"Maybe they went up this ladder," the boys heard Morgan cry.

"Let's check it out," said one of his followers.

T.J., Zack, and Charley ducked lower behind the metal box. If the other boys got up on the roof, they would be spotted almost immediately.

Suddenly, out of nowhere, a much deeper voice cut through the air. "YOU BOYS! GET OFF THAT LADDER!"

T.J. and Zack looked at one another. They knew that voice. That was Mr. Whitney, the school custodian. He had once gotten after T.J. for breaking a school window with a baseball, although it was proven to be an accident.

Mr. Whitney's voice was quite welcome to T.J.'s ears this time. He, Zack, and Charley grinned as they listened to Mr. Whitney chase Morgan and the others away from the ladder.

But the very next moment, their joy turned to alarm. A sudden clanging and banging from the side of the building meant only one thing—Mr. Whitney was taking down the ladder!

"What should we do?" Zack asked T.J. "If we don't tell him we're up here, he'll leave and we'll have no way to get down off the roof!"

"We can't tell Mr. Whitney we're up here!" T.J. looked at Zack as if he were crazy. "He'd kill us! Besides, I've been in enough trouble this week. I don't want to get in any more."

"But how do we get down?" Zack asked.

"We'll think of something," T.J. said lamely. But try as they would, the boys could find no other way off the roof. They watched the parking lot empty as, one by one, the teachers got into their cars and left.

"Now what?" Zack complained to T.J. "Are we going to spend the night up here?"

T.J. stared at his friend in anguish. Charley began to whimper. T.J. put a protective arm around his little brother. All three sat down and huddled against the metal fan box.

It was lonely and frightening being stuck up on a rooftop. T.J. gazed out over the empty playground. Now he wished Morgan had found him.

There was only one person who could help them now—one person who would know what to do. "Please, Lord Jesus," T.J. prayed silently, "please rescue us."

5

AN AWESOME RESCUE

The cold February wind whipped around their heads and through the boys' clothes, making it miserable on the rooftop. Minutes before, T.J. had walked all around the school roof, seeking a possible way down. He had rejected every possibility as too steep and dangerous, especially for his seven-year-old brother, Charley. After all, Charley had run into trouble just climbing the fence in the kindergarten courtyard. T.J. hated to think what might happen if Charley tried to climb down off of a roof.

"What we need now are those ropes that you tie onto the tops of buildings and then you hold onto the rope and kinda jump down the side of the building," said Zack, demonstrating with his hands and feet. "You know what it's called?"

"I know what you mean," replied T.J., "but I

can't think what it's called. I think it starts with a P."

"Rappelling," said Charley without batting an eye. "It's called rappelling."

"Right!" Zack looked surprised. "How'd you know that, Charley?"

Charley just smiled. T.J. rolled his eyes. He was used to Charley and his way of storing up odd bits of information just to throw at you when you least expected it, making him seem like a dopey little kid and a genius at the same time.

Suddenly, a distant noise attracted the boys' attention. An older woman had hurried out of the back door of a house whose yard backed up to part of the school's playground. She stood at the back fence and stared in the direction of the school. Quite suddenly, T.J. realized the woman was staring at him!

"HELP!" T.J. cried, jumping to his feet and waving his arms at the woman.

The woman waved her arm at the boys. "HOLD ON!" she called back over the fence.

"Awesome!" the boys cried. They slapped each other's hands and jumped around the roof.

"We're finally gonna be rescued," Zack sighed in relief, sitting back down to wait for the woman to somehow get them off the roof.

"Yeah, I knew we would be rescued," T.J. said confidently.

"What do you mean?" Zack asked skeptically. "How'd you know?"

"Because just a few minutes ago, I prayed and asked the Lord to send somebody to rescue us," came T.J.'s answer.

"Oh." Zack nodded and smiled.

Soon a car pulled into the parking lot of the school. The driver jumped out of the car and hurried over to the school building. It was the same woman who had waved at them from the fence.

"Don't worry, boys," she called up to them. "Help is on the way!"

Almost immediately, a police car, its lights flashing, pulled into the parking lot. A fire truck followed right behind it.

"Oh no!" T.J. and Zack covered their mouths in surprise at the sight of the big truck. Charley clapped his hands in glee.

To their further astonishment, a van bearing the sign CHANNEL 8 NEWS pulled in behind the fire truck. A man jumped out of the van and pointed a camera up at the boys.

"Boy T.J., when you pray for help, it looks like God answers!" Zack gave a low whistle.

"No kidding," T.J. nodded. Then he groaned. "There's Mrs. Larson." He pointed to the school principal who had just arrived in another car.

"I think we're in big trouble," Zack sighed.

The boys watched as the firefighters carried a long ladder from the truck and propped it up against the school building. Soon, a man's head appeared above the roof right in front of the boys. He climbed onto the roof and squatted down in front of the boys.

"Hello, boys," the firefighter smiled. "Is everybody all right up here?"

"Yeah," T.J. answered. Charley suddenly became very shy and ducked his head under T.J.'s arm.

The man asked the boys their names and ages. Zack and T.J. answered his questions. Charley continued to hide beneath T.J.'s arm.

The firefighter explained how he would stay with the boys to help them to the ladder, while another man would carry them down the ladder.

"Perhaps if you go first," the firefighter said to T.J., "your brother will see that everything is okay."

"Yeah, maybe." T.J. tried to pull Charley's head up, but the younger boy only buried himself deeper into T.J.'s jacket.

"Charley, what's the matter?" T.J. was becoming annoyed with his behavior. Charley was acting like such a dope.

"I don't get it," T.J. told the man. "He's not usually like this."

"That's okay," the firefighter replied. "He's awfully young to be stuck up on top of a building for so long."

"Maybe I should go first," Zack said. "Then Charley can stay with T.J. and watch me go down."

"Should we let Zack go first, Charley?" the firefighter tried to talk to the younger boy.

"Charley!" T.J. exclaimed when his brother didn't answer. "We have to get off the roof. Should I go first or Zack?"

At that, Charley raised his head and pointed at Zack. Then he ducked back under T.J.'s arm.

"No," T.J. pulled on his brother. "You have to watch Zack go down so you'll know what to do." But Charley would not raise his head again.

In the end, Zack went down the ladder first. Then the firefighter pulled Charley away from T.J. and carried him down the ladder. T.J. was the last to go. He would have enjoyed the exciting rescue much more if trouble had not been waiting for him at the bottom of the ladder.

Sure enough, as soon as T.J. reached the ground, he was placed in the backseat of the police car. Charley and Zack were there, and so was Mrs. Larson, the principal of the school.

Charley clung tightly to T.J. He seemed more afraid of the police car than he had been of the roof. After a few seconds in the car, T.J. understood why. The inside of the car looked very strange. A metal screen separated the front seat from the back. Large rifles stood within reach of the driver. Loud noises continually popped through the air from the police radio.

"Timothy John Fairbanks," Mrs. Larson

addressed T.J., "would you please tell me what you boys were doing up on the school roof? I asked Zack and he told me to ask you!"

T.J. squirmed uncomfortably. No one called him Timothy John unless he were in big trouble.

"Uh," T.J. stuttered, "we were, uh, just playing and, uh, we saw a ladder on the side of the building and we just sorta climbed up it."

"A ladder!" exclaimed Mrs. Larson. "What was a ladder doing at the side of the building?"

"I guess Mr. Whitney put it there," T.J. replied. "He took it away before we could climb back down."

Mrs. Larson looked surprised.

"You know, if anyone had been hurt, the school might have been held liable for leaving an unattended ladder against the school building," the police officer informed Mrs. Larson.

"Yes, I'm aware of that," Mrs. Larson said. "I'll speak to Mr. Whitney about it."

T.J. looked down at the floor in dismay. Not only were he, Zack, and Charley in trouble, but Mr. Whitney was in trouble too.

The police officer faced T.J., Zack, and Charley. She was a young woman with a very stern face.

"What you boys did today was extremely

dangerous," the police officer told them. "It was also against the law."

T.J. stiffened. Were they going to be arrested?

"If you ever again see a ladder propped up against a building, I want you to ignore it and walk away from it. Do you understand?" the officer asked the boys.

"Yes," said T.J. and Zack. Charley only hid his head.

"I have called your parents," the officer continued. "They should be here soon."

Indeed, within a minute the Fairbanks family van pulled up beside the police car. Out jumped T.J.'s mother and Zack's mother.

"T.J.!"

"Zack!"

"Charley!"

The mothers pulled the boys from the police car and looked them over.

"What happened?" Mother demanded as she held the now-sobbing Charley up against her. "We've been looking everywhere for you boys!"

The police officer told the mothers all that had happened. "You can see it for yourselves on the six o'clock news," she told them.

With a sigh, Mother loaded the boys into the van and drove home. When they reached the house, Father opened the front door.

"I was surprised to come home from work and find nobody here," he said with a worried face.

"Well," Mother looked at her watch, "in a few minutes, your questions will be answered on television."

"Huh?" Father replied.

Mother took Father into the kitchen where she explained what had happened. T.J. sat on a kitchen chair and listened, not daring to look at either parent. Charley sat beside him.

When Mother had finished, Father turned to T.J. and Charley.

"Can't you boys stay out of trouble two days running?" he asked.

"We didn't mean to get stuck on the roof," T.J. told him in a small voice.

"Uh huh," Father nodded, "and I suppose you didn't know it was wrong to climb a ladder that was standing at the side of the school building?"

"No, we knew that was wrong," T.J. admitted.

"Then why did you do it?" Father asked.

"I guess we thought it'd be fun," T.J. answered.

Mother stared at T.J. "Is that the only reason?" she questioned. "Is there more to the story that we should know about?"

How do mothers know these things? T.J. asked

himself. It was almost as if they were equipped with radar.

T.J. was tempted to tell his parents everything that had happened because of his bet with Morgan, but that would mean he'd have to tell them about wearing his clothes backward and getting in trouble with Mrs. Tuttle. He was already in a lot of trouble with his parents. How could he tell them about any more?

"No, there's nothing more to the story," T.J. told his mother.

"Then you boys are grounded for one week," Father replied, "with no television."

"I think you should write apology letters to Mrs. Larson, and the fire and police departments," said Mother, "telling them that you'll never do this again."

"Good idea," Father agreed. "You can write the letters after dinner," he told T.J. and Charley. "Now it's time to watch your rescue on television."

That evening, T.J. wrote the three letters that Mother had said to write. It took the entire evening.

"This is all Morgan's fault!" T.J. told himself. "Everything that's happened to me has been because of Morgan's stupid bet!"

T.J. angrily kicked his dresser, then quickly

rubbed his bruised foot. "I guess it really isn't all Morgan's fault," he finally admitted. "Some of it is my fault for making that dumb bet in the first place."

Now everyone was mad at him and things would be worse in the morning. Mrs. Tuttle would find out about the rescue. So would all the other kids. They would be sure to laugh at him for it.

"Oh, I'd rather be dead than go to school tomorrow," T.J. groaned and fell back on his bed.

6

CAUGHT IN THE ACT!

The next morning after breakfast, T.J. suddenly remembered something his teacher had told the class.

"Mom, I need a shoe box!" he shouted.

"Oh T.J., for heaven's sake. Why do you think of these things at the last moment? Why didn't you tell me that last night?" Mother asked.

"I had a lot on my mind last night," T.J. reminded her, "being stuck on the roof and all."

"That's for sure," Mother sighed. "I gave my last shoe box to Megan. Let's see if she still has it.

"Megan!" Mother called into the family room where Megan and Elizabeth were watching cartoons. "Do you still have the shoe box I gave you the other day?"

"Huh?" Megan ran to the kitchen. T.J. took one look at his five-year-old sister and laughed. She was wearing bright green leotards, Mickey

Mouse boxer shorts, and a neon pink bicycle helmet.

"Megan, where is the shoe box I gave you the other day?" Mother asked.

Megan looked from Mother to T.J. "You can't have it! It's my castle!" she told T.J.

"Where is it?" Mother asked, tapping her foot.

"In my room," Megan replied, "but it's Sleeping Beauty's castle."

"Oh brother," sighed T.J. He and Mother hurried upstairs to Megan's bedroom. Charley and Megan followed.

"Well, here it is," Mother pulled the shoe box out from under a pile of toys on the floor and handed it to T.J.

T.J. stared at the box in disgust. A crooked door and windows had been drawn on it with black marker. The rest had been scribbled pink.

"I can't take this to school! Don't you have another shoe box?" T.J. asked his mother.

"No, for some reason, they disappear as soon as I get them," Mother replied dryly.

"You can have one of mine if you don't mind dead bugs in it and air holes punched in the lid," Charley offered. "I got a whole bunch of shoe boxes for my bug collections."

"See what I mean?" Mother asked T.J.

With a heavy sigh, T.J., along with Mother and Megan, followed Charley into his bedroom.

"Which kind do you want?" Charley began pulling box after box out of his closet. "I got grasshopper boxes, cricket boxes, spider boxes..."

"I don't care!" T.J. cried, exasperated. "Just give me a box with the smallest holes in it."

"Let's see, that would be the spider box, cuz they have skinnier legs," Charley said as he handed a box to T.J. Pulling off the lid, T.J. discovered a clump of dead, dried-up black spiders.

"OOOUUUU YUCK!" Mother and Megan took one look and wrinkled up their noses.

"Charley, I don't even want to see what is in the other boxes," said Mother, "but this afternoon, I want you to dump everything that is dead into the trash. If there is anything alive in those boxes, please tell your father about it."

"Okay, Mom," said Charley.

"I guess I'll take this box to school," T.J. said after dumping the spiders into a wastebasket. "Dead spiders have got to be better than Sleeping Beauty's castle," he teased his little sister.

"They are not!" Megan cried.

Upon reaching school that morning, T.J. was glad not to find a group of boys waiting for him

in the schoolyard. When he and Zack walked into the classroom, however, cheers and whistles met their ears.

"We saw you guys on television last night!" the students shouted.

Mrs. Tuttle was concerned. "I'm glad you are all right," she told T.J. and Zack. "Climbing up on the school roof was a dangerous thing to do."

"We won't do it again," the boys assured her.

At lunch, the third-grade boys talked about T.J.'s and Zack's escape to the school rooftop.

"We thought you had gone up the ladder,"

Morgan told T.J., "but Mr. Whitney wouldn't let us go up and see. As it turned out, you got in more trouble than if we would have caught you!" he and the others laughed.

"That's for sure," T.J. agreed.

"Why did you run away from us anyway?" Anthony wanted to know. "Were you chicken?"

"I just didn't feel like being hassled," T.J. replied in a low voice.

"I think you were scared of us," Anthony teased.

"Anthony, shut up!" cried Zack.

"Anthony, yesterday we noticed how well you climbed the fence that surrounds the kindergarten courtyard," T.J. said, smiling mockingly at Anthony.

Anthony turned bright. "His pant leg was torn all the way up!" the others snickered.

"Since you ran out on us yesterday, you're gonna have to make up for it," Morgan told T.J. All sounds of laughter vanished from the table.

T.J. frowned at Morgan. Was this never going to end? "What do you mean?" he asked Morgan.

"You can make it up by getting me some chocolate milk up there in the cafeteria line," Morgan pointed toward the front of the cafeteria.

"I don't have any extra money for chocolate milk," T.J. told Morgan.

"I didn't say buy it," Morgan replied.

"You mean you want me to steal milk for you?" T.J. said, a shocked look on his face.

"There's nothing to it," Morgan replied. "Just take your tray up there and pretend you're throwing away your trash. Then, grab a milk carton. It's sitting right at the end of the line by the trash barrel."

"Yeah, but . . ." T.J. started to object.

"Go on, Chicken," the other boys teased.

"What if the cafeteria people see me?" T.J. asked.

"Do it when nobody's looking," was the reply.

"It's too risky," T.J. said. "I'm in enough trouble."

"We always knew you were yellow," the boys jeered. "Squawk! Bawk! Chicken!" They flapped their arms up and down like chickens.

"C'mon, T.J., you made the bet," Morgan insisted.

"Oh, okay!" T.J. exclaimed angrily. "You guys just want me to get kicked out of school!"

Stomping to the front part of the cafeteria, T.J. set his tray of empty dishes down by the big metal container full of milk cartons. While pretending to throw away his trash in the nearby barrel, T.J. grabbed a carton of chocolate milk and set it down among the empty dishes on his tray. He then carried the tray and the milk back to the table full of boys.

"Hooray for T.J.!" the boys all cried as T.J. handed Morgan the carton of chocolate milk.

"Aw, it was easy," T.J. shrugged his shoulders and tried to appear calm when actually his heart felt like it was racing a million miles a second.

"If it was so easy, how 'bout getting some more?" Morgan grinned wickedly at T.J.

"Yeah, go get all of us some chocolate milk, T.J.," the boys laughed.

"No, once was enough," said T.J.

"Aw, come on, Chicken! Bawk! Squawk!"

T.J. was undecided. He knew stealing chocolate milk was wrong. Yet the boys were calling him chicken. In the end, he went back up to the cafeteria line with his tray. He stole another carton of milk with no problem, but the third time he tried it proved to be disastrous.

As he reached for the milk, a white-haired cafeteria worker suddenly appeared out of nowhere and grabbed his hand. The woman's eyes flashed angrily at T.J. With her other hand, she whacked a stalk of celery down hard on the counter. Bits of it flew into T.J.'s face.

"Don't you know it's wrong to steal milk?" the woman shouted at T.J. She called to the teacher on duty. "This boy's stealing milk! I saw him take another carton just a couple of minutes ago."

T.J.'s face grew hot and his knees went weak as a hush filled the cafeteria. All eyes were on T.J. Humiliated, T.J. let the teacher lead him from the room and down the hall to the principal's office.

Terrified, T.J. waited to see Mrs. Larson. Just the night before, he and Zack had climbed up on the school roof. Now he had been caught stealing! Mrs. Larson was going to be dreadfully angry. Oh, why had he done such a stupid thing?

7

THE STRONGEST KIND OF STRONG

The door of the principal's office opened slowly. Mrs. Larson asked T.J. to come inside her office.

T.J. got up off the chair in the outer office. The pressure had been too much for him. He had not been able to hold back his tears. His eyes were red and his nose was running. He stumbled through the door into Mrs. Larson's office.

"T.J., I can't believe it," Mrs. Larson exclaimed. "Did you really steal milk from the cafeteria?"

Miserably, T.J. nodded his head. Fresh tears rolled down his cheeks. He couldn't speak. A huge lump blocked his throat.

"Why in the world did you steal that milk?" Mrs. Larson asked. "I know your parents have taught you better than that."

The mention of his parents made T.J. even more miserable. They were going to be so upset when they heard about this.

Mrs. Larson handed T.J. some tissue. He wiped his eyes and blew his nose. In a shaky voice, T.J. told the principal everything that had happened between him and Morgan during the past week.

"It sounds like you've had a pretty rough time," Mrs. Larson said after hearing the whole story. "Do you see where bragging and betting lead? Maybe you'll think twice before you make such a bet again."

"I'll never do that again!" T.J. exclaimed. "It was a really stupid thing to do."

"Yes, it made you do some very bad things," Mrs. Larson said. "Stealing is a serious offense. Ordinarily, we suspend students who are caught stealing. However, because the other boys put you up to it, and because I don't think you'd have done it on your own, you will not be suspended. But I will have to call your parents."

T.J. sighed. At least it would all be over soon.

T.J.'s mother came to the school and talked with Mrs. Larson. She took T.J. home for the rest of the afternoon.

"What have you learned from all of this, T.J.," Mother asked after T.J. had told her all about the bet with Morgan.

"Well," T.J. replied, "I learned that making the bet was wrong."

"Why was it wrong?" Mother asked.

"Because I lost and had to do all those bad things," answered T.J.

"Yes, you did bad things and got in trouble," agreed Mother, "but making the bet in the first place was wrong. It doesn't matter whether you won or lost the bet. Betting is wrong."

"Oh?" T.J. frowned. "Why?"

"Because when you make a bet against someone," replied Mother, "either you or the other person is going to get hurt. When you bet against someone, you are trying to beat that person. That's not right. That's not what Jesus taught us to do. How can we love other people if we bet against them?"

"But I didn't bet money or anything like that," said T.J. "I just bet that I was stronger than Morgan."

"Yes, and you lost the bet and got hurt because of it," Mother reminded him. "If Morgan had lost the bet, he would have been the one who got hurt. Someone is always the loser when you make a bet. Do you see what I mean?"

"Yeah, I see," T.J. replied.

"Now, let me ask you a question," said Mother. "Do you really think that whoever does the most chin-ups is the strongest?"

"Yeah," T.J. frowned. "Don't you think so?"

"No, not really," Mother answered. "Doing lots of chin-ups might show that you are strong physically, but there's a better kind of strong than that—it's the strongest kind of strong."

"The strongest kind of strong?" T.J. looked puzzled. "What do you mean?"

"I mean being strong in the Lord," Mother replied. "I mean placing all your strength in the Lord. Do you remember the story of David and Goliath?"

"Sure," said T.J. "Goliath was a mean giant and David was a boy who decided to fight him."

"And what happened?" asked Mother.

"David shot a rock from his slingshot at Goliath's forehead and killed him," T.J. told her.

"How do you think that happened?" Mother asked. "Was David stronger than Goliath?"

"No," T.J. said. "David was a lot smaller than Goliath."

"Then how did David manage to kill Goliath?" Mother wanted to know.

"Maybe he was just lucky," T.J. shrugged.

"No, he wasn't just lucky," Mother smiled. "When Goliath yelled at David, called him a weakling, and said he was going to kill him and feed him to the wild beasts, do you know what David answered?"

"No," said T.J.

"David said, 'I come to you in the name of the Lord. Today the Lord will deliver you into my hands, and everyone will know that there is a God in Israel!'

"You see," Mother went on, "David was strong in the Lord. He placed all his strength in the Lord. He trusted the Lord to protect him and to help him fight the giant."

"Yeah," T.J. nodded. He had always liked the story of how little David had defeated big Goliath.

"You can be strong in the Lord too," Mother told T.J. "You can fight for the Lord just as David did."

"How do you fight for the Lord?" T.J. asked.

"By fighting against evil," answered Mother. "Every time you take a stand against wrong and do what's right, you are doing battle for the Lord."

"Like refusing to make bets?" T.J. asked.

"Exactly!" said Mother. "Then, you are in God's army just like David."

"Really?" T.J. whistled. "Then, I could be the strongest kind of strong?"

"You bet!" said Mother, and they both laughed.

T.J. spent the rest of the afternoon alone in his bedroom. When Father got home, he went upstairs immediately.

"Mother told me all about what happened today," he said to T.J. as he entered his bedroom. "I wish you would have come to us in the first place and told us you were having problems. Then we could have helped you."

"Yeah," T.J. agreed. "I wanted to tell you and Mom everything, but I was afraid to tell you about all the trouble I got into at school."

"But can't you see that by waiting to tell us, the trouble just got worse?" asked Father. "That's what happens with trouble. If you don't take care of it right away, it only gets worse."

"I see that now," T.J. replied. "I'll try to do

better, Dad," he promised.

"I know you will, T.J." Father patted his shoulder.

After Father left, T.J. got out the box of valentines his mother had given him. He did not want to get in any further trouble by not having his valentines ready.

T.J. looked over the valentines. They weren't too bad. One was of a basketball player that said, "Slam dunk! Have a super day!" Another had a baseball player that said, "You're a sure hit!" On another, a man with muscular arms was hitting a bell with a sledgehammer. It said, "You're tops, Valentine!" T.J.'s favorite was of a soccer player that said, "My goal is to make you my valentine!" Maybe he'd give Morgan the soccer valentine just to make him mad.

T.J. had just begun to work on the valentines when a low knock sounded on his door. Opening it, T.J. found Charley crouched outside the door.

"Quick, T.J., I need your help!" Charley hissed.

"I can't come out of my room," T.J. reminded him. "I got in big trouble today."

"I know, but it's an emergency!" Charley begged. "Just come down to the bathroom for a minute."

"The bathroom?" T.J. frowned. "Why?"

"You'll see," Charley said mysteriously.

Grumbling, T.J. followed his brother down to

the second-floor bathroom. To his surprise, Megan and Elizabeth were waiting there for him and Charley.

"What is this?" T.J. joked. "A town meeting?"

"It's not funny," Charley told him. He flung open the cabinet door under the sink. "Look!"

T.J. stared in disbelief at the mess under the sink. The U-shaped metal pipe that normally carried the water from the sink to the drain pipes, had been pulled apart and lay in a twisted heap. Water covered the bottom of the cabinet, soaking through everything that had been stored there, including several very soggy rolls of toilet paper. The water was beginning to overflow onto the floor.

"What happened?" T.J. cried in alarm.

"Well, Elizabeth dropped her ring down the drain in the sink and Charley's Repair Service took apart the pipe to try to find the ring."

"Why is there water everywhere?" T.J. demanded.

"I couldn't find the ring in the pipe so I tried to flush it out with water. I forgot there wasn't pipe under the sink to catch the water, and it ran out onto the floor," Charley explained.

T.J. slapped his forehead with his hand. How did Charley manage to turn everything into a disaster?

"You are a walking, talking disaster!" T.J. told Charley. "Instead of making a movie about dogs, somebody ought to make a movie about you and call it 'One Hundred and One Disasters'!"

Megan and Elizabeth laughed.

"T.J., just help me get everything back together before Mom and Dad find out," Charley begged.

T.J. shook his head. "You know, Charley, this reminds me of the doorknob incident. You got me in a lot of trouble over that one, and I'm not about to make the same mistake again. As Dad says, 'I may be dumb, but I'm not stupid!' "

With that, T.J. turned and called down the stairs, "Mom! Dad! You better come up here quick!"

Charley groaned and fell to the bathroom floor as Mother and Father ran up the stairs.

"What's the matter?" his parents asked at once.

"Charley's Repair Service strikes again," said T.J. He showed them the cabinet under the sink.

"OH NO!" Mother and Father both cried.

"I'll get some towels," T.J. ran to the linen closet.

T.J. and Mother mopped up the cabinet while Father tried to fit the pipe back in place. Charley hauled the wet toilet paper to the trash.

Finally, Father gave up. "This pipe is too bent

up. I'm going to have to call a plumber in the morning to come and fix it."

After listening to Charley's explanation of his latest disaster, Mother asked, "T.J., how did you know about this? I thought you were in your room."

"I was in my room, but Charley told me there was an emergency in the bathroom. He wanted to get it back together again before you found out."

"What did you tell him?" Father asked.

"I told him this was just the same kind of disaster as the doorknob incident and I might be dumb but I wasn't stupid!" T.J. grinned at his parents.

Mother and Father laughed. "You did the right thing, T.J.," Father praised him. "As a reward, you may watch television tonight."

Happily, T.J. ran back upstairs to finish the valentines. He would give Morgan the one with the muscular man with a sledgehammer. He knew Morgan would like that one better than the soccer player. T.J. was tired of making people angry—even Morgan.

8

UP AGAINST THE GIANT!

The next morning, T.J. approached the school nervously. Not only might Mrs. Tuttle be mad at him for stealing milk from the cafeteria, but the third-grade boys might be angry because he told Mrs. Larson about their part in the affair. He was afraid Morgan might try to get back at him in some way.

Sure enough, when T.J., Zack, and Aaron entered the school, they found the boys waiting for them, with Morgan at the front of the group.

As he walked toward Morgan, T.J. felt an urge to use one of his soccer fakes, dodge the big boy, and make an all-out run to his classroom. He held his ground, however, and waited for Morgan to speak. To his great astonishment, Morgan began to apologize.

"T.J., I'm really sorry about yesterday and all the trouble you got into," Morgan told him. "I guess our bet got a little out of hand."

"Uh, that's okay," T.J. replied awkwardly.

"I had a long talk with Mrs. Larson about it yesterday," Morgan told him. "She told me about your problems at home and how upset your parents have been about all the trouble you've been getting into. I didn't think about that."

"Oh, well," T.J. smiled. "At least it's over now."

The boys walked together into the classroom. Mrs. Tuttle smiled at T.J. and said, "Good morning," as if nothing had happened. T.J. wondered if she, too, had talked with Mrs. Larson.

When he reached his desk, T.J. was surprised to see sitting on one corner of his desk a wonderfully decorated valentine box. Different colored soccer balls mixed with hearts covered the outside. The initials "T.J." and a picture of a boy in soccer uniform stood on the top of the box.

"WOW!" T.J. whistled. Who had decorated the valentine box? Because he had been sent home early yesterday by the principal, he had not been able to do it himself.

"Your friends got together and decorated your valentine box, T.J.," Mrs. Tuttle told him.

"Yeah, Morgan and I cut out all the soccer balls," Anthony said with a sheepish grin.

"We pasted them on the box," said the other boys.

"We made the hearts," said Ashley and Jennifer.

"Aaron and I made the boy kicking the soccer ball," grinned Zack.

"I put on your initials," smiled Mrs. Tuttle. "We wanted you to know that we are your friends."

"Gee, thanks!" T.J. replied, embarrassed by all the attention. He sat down, red-faced but happy, in his chair.

Everything had turned out so well. Mrs. Tuttle was not angry with him. Morgan, Anthony, and the other boys were his friends. Even Ashley and Jennifer had done something nice for him.

Because the weather was cold and rainy, recess was held in the gymnasium. Ms. Springate, the gym teacher, divided everyone into several teams for relay races.

T.J. was made captain of his team. They had a good chance of winning. There was Zack, a very fast runner, and Mark, also pretty fast. The girls on the team, Jessie, Wendy, and Keri, were all good runners. The only problem was a boy named Jeffrey. He did not go out for sports and was not much of an athlete.

T.J. carefully decided the order of the runners.

Zack would run first, Jeffrey second, Wendy third, Mark fourth, Jessie fifth, Keri sixth, and T.J. would run as anchor.

The first runners for each team stepped up to the starting line. Morgan's team stood next to T.J's team. It looked as though Morgan would run anchor for his team. T.J. happily noticed that Anthony was on Morgan's team. Anthony was a very slow runner.

"ON YOUR MARK! GET SET! GO!" Ms. Springate shouted.

The first runners took off. They had to run the length of the gym and back again. Each carried a lightweight baton to pass to the next runner on their team.

T.J. smiled as Zack easily pulled ahead of the other runners to start their team off first in the relays. Jeffrey, however, the team's second runner, lost ground as he trudged down the length of the gym and back. Wendy made up for lost time and so did Mark. While watching his own team, T.J. also kept an eye on the other teams. It looked like Morgan's team and T.J.'s team were battling for first place.

T.J. breathed a little easier as Jessie, the team's fifth runner, pulled way ahead of the others. But he gasped in horror a few moments later when

Keri, runner number six, tripped and fell to the ground. The runner from Morgan's team passed her by and remained in the lead on the homestretch.

"Oh no!" T.J. told himself. "Morgan's going to get a big head start on me." Even though he and Morgan were friends now, T.J. hated to have to lose to him again. But could he come from behind and beat the big muscular boy? The way T.J. saw it, there was only one thing to do.

"Dear Lord Jesus," T.J. prayed desperately, "You helped David beat the giant, Goliath. Please help me beat Morgan. Amen."

When Keri passed the baton to T.J., he exploded off the starting line like a rocket. With his feet flying toward the far wall of the gym, he had only one thought—beat Morgan! He did not look to the right or to the left, but kept his eyes straight ahead. He ran as his soccer coach had taught him—an all-out sprint toward the goal, every muscle driving him forward, stretching for the victory.

Somehow, even after starting from behind, T.J. reached the far wall the same time Morgan did. With a lightning-quick turn, T.J. propelled himself back to the starting line, his feet scarcely touching the floor. He finished the race a good five feet in front of Morgan!

"WHOOOOOOOEEEEE!" Zack screamed louder than anyone else. He knew what it meant to T.J. to beat Morgan. He leaped high in the air to smack T.J.'s outstretched hand in a high five.

Seconds later, Morgan congratulated T.J. "Wrestlers might have stronger arms, but soccer players have faster feet!" he told T.J.

T.J. laughed happily. He was the winner today. He had beaten the giant!

"Thank You, Lord," he whispered.

Still excited about the relay races, T.J., Zack, and Aaron talked about nothing else as they walked home after school. T.J. could hardly wait to tell Mother and Father about his win over Morgan.

When they reached T.J.'s house, a big white truck was parked in the driveway. On the side of the truck was printed, TOM COOPER'S PLUMBING AND REPAIR SERVICE.

"Hmmmmm," T.J. nudged his younger brother, "I wonder why that truck is here?"

"What do you mean? What does it say?" the first grader asked.

After T.J. told him, Charley let out a whoop of excitement and ran into the house. Shaking his head at his brother's behavior, T.J. said good-bye to Zack and Aaron and followed Charley inside. He met Mother in the kitchen and told her all about the race with Morgan and how he had won.

"I asked the Lord to help me like He helped David beat Goliath, and He did!" T.J. said excitedly.

"I'm not surprised," Mother smiled. "The Lord always helps His soldiers."

"Am I really one of His soldiers?" T.J. asked hopefully.

"There's no doubt about it," nodded Mother.

Just then, Charley burst through the kitchen from the garage and bounded up the stairway. He was wearing his overalls. Tools stuck out of the pockets. A backward ball cap and Father's goggles were balanced on his head. "Charleys Repare Serviss" was scribbled on the back of Charley's T-shirt.

T.J. and Mother looked at one another in alarm. "OH NO!" they cried. Running upstairs, they found Charley squatting down beside the plumber to watch as he replaced the bent and twisted pipes that belonged under the bathroom sink.

Both Mother and T.J. grabbed Charley at once and hauled him downstairs to the kitchen.

"But I only want to watch the plumber fix the pipes!" Charley bawled.

"No way!" Mother and T.J. told him. Then they all burst into laughter.

Amen.

T.J.

Pet snakes.
Racing cars.
Soccer.

T.J.'s life is filled with all sorts of adventures. Whether he's trying to figure out how to get along with a bully on the swim team or how to get off the rooftop of the school building, T.J. learns that God always has the answer and can help him deal with even the worst of problems.

Be sure to read all the books in the T.J. series:

The Pet That Never Was
The Fastest Car in the County
Trouble in the Deep End
Hero for a Season
Master of Disaster

by Nancy Simpson Levene

It's Alex!

"Brussels Sprouts!"

Every kid gets into the predicaments Alex does—ones that start out small and mushroom. Whether it's figuring out how to replace lost shoelaces or trying to win a contest, you'll laugh along with Alex as she learns that God always loves her, no matter what she's done.

Be sure to read all the books in the Alex series:

Shoelaces and Brussels Sprouts
French Fry Forgiveness
Hot Chocolate Friendship
Peanut Butter and Jelly Secrets
Mint Cookie Miracles
Cherry Cola Champions
The Salty Scarecrow Solution
Peach Pit Popularity
T-Bone Trouble
Grapefruit Basket Upset
Apple Turnover Treasure
Crocodile Meatloaf

by Nancy Simpson Levene